Beautiful Ballerina

by Marilyn Nelson

photographs by Susan Kuklin

SCHOLASTIC PRESS / NEW YORK

Acknowledgments:

I'd like to thank my editor, Andrea Davis Pinkney; my agent, Regina Brooks;

and my friend R. B. Wilkenfield for their support and assistance. — MN

Library of Congress Cataloging-in-Publication Data

Nelson, Marilyn, 1946-
Beautiful ballerina / by Marilyn Nelson ; photographs by Susan Kuklin. — 1st ed.   p. cm.
ISBN-13: 978-0-545-08920-3
ISBN-10: 0-545-08920-4
1. Ballet—Juvenile literature. I. Title.   GV1787.5.N45 2009   792.8—dc22   2009009135

Printed in Singapore   46
First edition, September 2009

The text type was set in Canterbury Old Style.
Book design by Lillie Mear

To Maja and to Maya. You are the dance — MN

For Bailey and all past, present, and future dancers — SK

Beautiful ballerina,

you are slender,

straight-legged,

high-arched, symmetrical,

with strong this-little-piggie toes.

You are

poised,

graceful,

flexible,

elegant.

Your beauty invites

bravissimos.

Beautiful ballerina,

you are

the dance.

The Ancestors have

produced a swan.

You wear the slaves' genes

with nobility.

You dance the dreams

of generations gone

so beautifully,

blossoms open on

the family tree.

Beautiful
ballerina,
you are

the dance.

But a ballerina is not

made of genes alone.

Your physical grace and

strength

    must be matched by

strength of will.

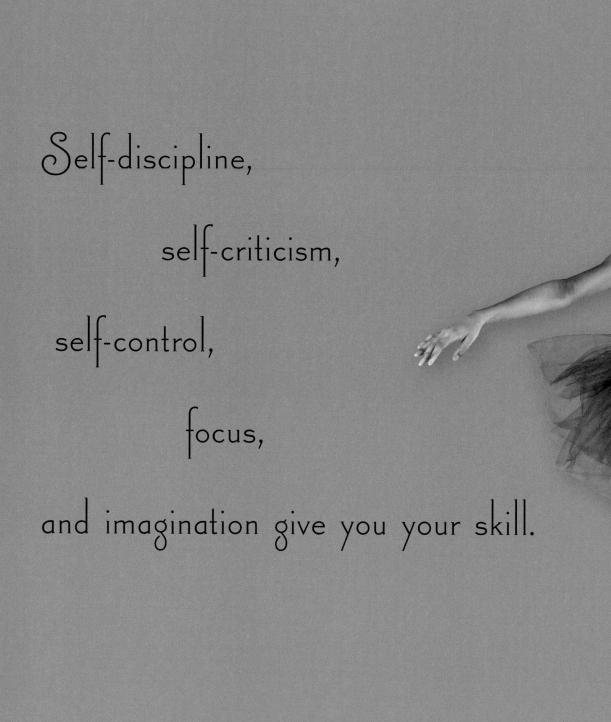

Self-discipline,

self-criticism,

self-control,

focus,

and imagination give you your skill.

Beautiful ballerina,

you are

the dance.

To the traditions

arabesque,

jetés, and

you bring a tiny

juju and beautiful joy

of *port de bras* and

of *pirouettes,*

pas de deux,

hint of Africanness,

danced in your every move.

Beautiful ballerina,
you are the dance.

En point in *tutu* when the music tinkles,

you're a transmitter of twitter,

and then you sweep into a leap.

You dance madness

and sadness,

fairies,

love,

betrayal.

You plant enchantment on the planet

with every step.

Beautiful
ballerina,

you are

the dance.

You hear both outer and inner music.

You s t r e t c h the laws of gravity.

Beautiful ballerina,

you are the dance.

Dance all of the people free.

Beautiful ballerina,

you are the dance.

Special thanks to Dance Theatre of Harlem and the following individuals for their creative support of this book, which would not have been possible without their grace, artistic direction, and style.

Arthur Mitchell, the primary founder of Dance Theatre of Harlem, was the first African American to become a permanent member of the New York City Ballet, where, in 1955, he rose quickly to principal dancer and electrified audiences with his performances. Because of his renown—and the many opportunities he had been given to study and perform ballet—Mr. Mitchell felt he had been able to change the world of dance, and he wanted to provide similar opportunities to others. Toward that end, Mr. Mitchell founded Dance Theatre of Harlem in 1969 with his mentor and ballet instructor, Karel Shook. Mr. Mitchell continues to be the driving force behind Dance Theatre of Harlem's mission to provide dance instruction and performance of the highest quality.

Endalyn Taylor co-choreographed the ballet that appears in this book along with photographer Susan Kuklin. She is the director of Dance Theatre of Harlem. Ms. Taylor, also a dancer, studied with the Joffrey Ballet, Pennsylvania Ballet, and Dance Theatre of Harlem School. In 1984, Ms. Taylor joined Dance Theatre of Harlem's professional company and became a principal dancer in 1993. She has performed in several Broadway productions, including *Carousel*, *The Lion King*, and *Aida*.

Doris attends the Dance Theatre of Harlem Community program. Doris's favorite activities are playing in the park, swimming, making friends, puzzles, and piano lessons.

Jalen studies piano and attends Dance Theatre of Harlem's Pre-Professional program. Jalen loves to dance because she says it expresses her feelings.

Raven M. loves basketball, track, reading, and social studies. She is a student in Dance Theatre of Harlem's Pre-Professional program.

Raven B. joined Dance Theatre of Harlem in 2006, and hopes to one day be a principal dancer with Dance Theatre of Harlem's professional company. Raven is an advanced student in Dance Theatre of Harlem's Pre-Professional program.

Dance Theatre of Harlem has been hailed by *The New York Times* as "one of ballet's most exciting undertakings."

Shortly after the assassination of the Reverend Dr. Martin Luther King, Jr., Arthur Mitchell was inspired to start a school that would offer children—especially those in Harlem, the community in which he was born—the opportunity to study classical dance.

Dance Theatre of Harlem's primary purpose is to maintain a ballet company of artists of both African American and diverse backgrounds, who perform the most demanding repertory at the highest level of quality. In addition, Dance Theatre of Harlem seeks to maintain a world-class organization that trains young people in classical ballet and the allied arts, and provides education and community outreach programs that offer positive role models, instruction, and introduction to the arts.